JAKE IN SPACE
ROBOT GAMES

D1364433

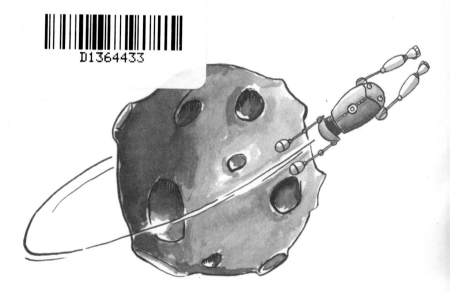

Candice Lemon-Scott
Illustrated by Celeste Hulme

NEW FRONTIER PUBLISHING

Whoosh! A robot in a jet-powered winged suit flew straight past Jake and his friends. It looked like a cross between a person and a plane. Jake could smell the burning fuel as the robot shot upwards. The heat from the jets was so intense it almost burned the skin on his face.

Zoom! Another robot came out of nowhere. Jake jumped as it roared by, making him spill his super-fizz swurpie all over himself.

The rainbow-coloured fizzy bubbles started popping all over his pants, leaving a wet, sticky mess.

'Great!' he mumbled, pulling an instant-dry cloth from his shirt pocket.

He was busy trying to wipe his pants clean when Rory nudged him. Following his gaze skywards, Jake's jaw dropped open. Eight jet-powered robots had formed a circle in midair. They hovered, wings almost touching. Then they began to spin, faster and faster, until it looked like a black disc had formed in the sky.

A computerised voice boomed through the arena: 'Welcome to the Twelfth Forty-Year Robot Games!'

The crowd cheered loudly – the arena was a volcano erupting. Jake looked around. There were over a hundred levels in the Robot Games arena. It was so huge that Jake could hardly see the crowd on the other side.

2

He could only make out the flashes of cheer flares going off, bursting out in the colours of the different robot teams. Hover taxis zipped by every now and then, moving vertically or horizontally as they transported people around the arena. It was too huge for some of the spectators to even walk to the nearest toilets. People had come from all over the solar system to watch the Games.

Jake and his friends – Skye, Rory and Milly – had been dropped off early that morning by their parents so they could see the whole day of events. They had been given their tickets as prizes for winning the Rocket Battles space car race, and for weeks they had been learning all about the Games from their families and at school. Mostly, the events were a chance for the inventors, engineers and designers to show off their robot creations – and they showed off in spectacular style.

Every seat was now full, except the empty one next to Jake. He wondered what had happened to that ticket holder. No-one lucky enough to get a ticket missed the Games. Fans without a ticket could watch the Games from one of the gigantic sky screens put up throughout the solar system, and huge crowds gathered to watch the day's events wherever they could.

The Robot Games were already better than he'd imagined, and this was only the opening display. He could see that his friends were just as amazed. Rory, Milly and Skye – who had also been on the winning Rocket Battles team – were all staring up at the sky.

The jet-powered robots stopped spinning, then dived towards the arena at an amazing speed. Bright red and orange flames shot from their backs, leaving eight streaks of colour in the sky. They darted around the arena one last

4

time before disappearing through the mid-level competitor bay. The crowd cheered.

'Wow! That was incredible,' Rory gasped.

'Cool wing design,' Skye added.

'What's up next?' Milly asked.

Jake opened his notepod and typed in a search. A 3D image of robots parading the grounds came up.

'The opening parade, and then ...' He flicked his fingers over the screen and a miniature image of the first robot event appeared. 'Robot high jump.'

Rory looked over Jake's shoulder at the screen. 'Whoa! Spring-loaded – yeah!'

'Not that difficult considering such technology has existed for centuries.'

The four of them turned. Henry, their friend – and cyborg – sat down in the empty spot beside Jake. He opened a packet of some kind of popping snack Jake had never seen before and poured it straight into his mouth. Jake stared at the skin on Henry's cheeks ballooning out in places as huge balls of popcorn exploded in his mouth.

'Would you care for some?' Henry mumbled, holding the bag out to Jake.

'Um ... what is it?' Jake asked, frowning.

'Gob Pop,' Henry replied.

'Um, no thanks,' Jake said, shaking his head.

'I didn't know *you* got a ticket too,' Rory whined.

Henry sucked in his cheeks. Jake wasn't sure if it was because Rory had upset him, or if it was the effect of the popcorn, but he looked pretty weird.

'I was in the space race team too,' Henry said, 'in case you are experiencing a lapse of memory.'

'*You're* the one who had a memory lapse – when you forgot to mention we were only

6

in the Rocket Battles race to save Mars – *my planet!*'

'I was sworn to secrecy,' Henry said, his cheeks puffing out like balloons.

'Guys! You're spoiling the fun of the Games,' Milly said.

Henry's cheeks went back to normal. 'Sorry. Gob Pop?' he said, offering the bag to the girls.

'No thanks,' Milly and Skye said together.

'It is an interesting taste sensation,' Henry said before shoving another handful into his mouth.

Jake noticed that something else was different about Henry too. He just couldn't figure out what it was.

'Why did you get here late if you already had a ticket?' Jake asked.

'I was having an upgrade,' Henry said. He opened his arm panel and showed them his brand new, super-shiny, super-techno gear.

He closed it again, grinned and tapped his head proudly. 'I was given this special cap to wear also. Quite smart, I think.'

That was what was different about him. Jake was so used to seeing Henry with his slicked-down black hair. It reminded him of the no-gravity hair wax Henry used. Though it was the stinkiest stuff ever, it sure had helped them stop the Neptune Goons from blowing up Mars in the Rocket Battles. Jake couldn't believe it had only been a few months ago that the Central Intergalactic Agency – the CIA – had sent him and his friends on a mission so secret they didn't even know they were in it. Clearly Rory had remembered, though. He was still angry with Henry for not telling them about the mission.

At least today they could enjoy the Games without wondering what secret mission the CIA had sent them on, since their tickets were

8

the prize for solving that mystery. Henry was already enjoying his prize too. Or at least the noisy snack he was loudly munching on.

'Where did you get that Gob Pop from?' Jake asked.

But Henry couldn't say any more – the popcorn had started exploding inside his mouth once again.

The great gates halfway up the side of the arena opened with a screech that was so ear-piercing that everyone covered their ears. When it finally stopped the Games commentary began.

'We welcome the teams of the Robot Games.'

Jake heard the clunking of metal on metal as the first robot team marched through the gates. Painted bright yellow, their metallic bodies shone like a burning sun as they entered the arena and made their way around the hovering competitor ring. They walked around in tighter and tighter circles until they formed a circle in the centre. At the same time the robot creator team was shown on giant floating screens around the arena. All the creator groups had to be made up of a man, a woman, a boy and a girl. The yellow team's four creators looked like they hadn't washed or eaten for months. Their hair was matted and the man had a full beard. They were all skinny and dressed alike. Their overalls might have once been white but were now a dull grey and marked with pen, food and other disgusting-looking things. They waved bony fingers as though they could see the crowd in front of them.

Next, the orange robots emerged. Their creators were the complete opposite of the first group. This lot had slicked-back hair and

10

clean, pressed suits. The orange robots took their place in a circle around the yellow team.

The rest of the robot teams came out until there was a swirl covering the floating ring. It looked like a rainbow snail shell. The last team's creators stared out from the screen. They all wore thick glasses and had serious faces.

Finally, the floating screens disappeared and the robots saluted the crowd. The hovering competitor ring moved in a whirl of colour around the arena until finally it drifted slowly to the ground. The robots unfurled and ran off, waving flags the colour of their teams.

'Let the Games begin. May the best team win.'

The announcer's voice faded away and the arena began to shake as the crowd clapped and pounded their feet to mark the start of the Games. Jake looked over at Skye and she smiled at him. This was going to be the greatest thing he'd ever seen. He just knew it.

MEDICAL CENTRE

2

The first event in the Robot Games was the robot high jump. A glowing laser light shone from the centre of the arena to measure the height of the jumps. The first robot jumped so high it became just a tiny speck in the air above Jake. They all watched, amazed – except Henry, who chomped through handfuls of Gob Pop. As the second robot entered the field, Henry put yet another fistful of Gob Pop in his mouth.

Rory rolled his eyes.

'Where are you getting all that popcorn from?' Jake said.

Henry opened up his backpack. It was completely full of bags of Gob Pop. The cyborg swallowed again. He touched his stomach. It was shaking from all the popcorn that was still popping.

'You're going to make yourself sick eating all that,' Skye said.

'It is indeed making me a little bit thirsty,' he said. 'I shall go and purchase a drink.'

But when Henry went to get up he couldn't stand. Actually he couldn't do anything. He had shut down.

'What's wrong with him?' Milly asked, tapping him gently on the shoulder.

'He's probably just shut himself down to recharge,' Jake answered. He checked Henry's battery level but it was still at eighty per cent.

He opened the panel on Henry's arm. Even though it was shiny and new, everything seemed to be working okay. All the wires were in place and the control panel was lit up as normal.

Skye stood in front of Henry. She put her hand in front of his mouth, then over his chest.

'Lung function okay. Heart beating. He seems to be ... frozen?' she said. Then she put her hand over his stomach. 'The popcorn's still popping in his tummy, though – I can feel it.'

'What are we going to do with him?' Milly said. 'We can't just leave him like this.'

'Why not?' Rory answered.

The three friends glared at him. Jake agreed with the girls. They had to get him out of the arena, and to a doctor, or to whatever place it was you took cyborgs to when they weren't working properly.

'We need to get him to the arena medical

centre,' Skye said. 'I passed the sign when we came in – it's down one of the tunnels near the main gates.'

'How are we going to do that?' Milly asked.

'We'll have to carry him.'

Milly and Skye put their hands under Henry's shoulders. Jake held him under one leg. After a bit of bribing with a pack of space jubes, Rory put his hand beneath Henry's other leg.

'Okay, on the count of three we'll lift him,' Jake said.

The others nodded.

'One, two, three ... *lift*.'

They couldn't lift Henry. In fact, they couldn't move him at all. He was far too heavy, even for all four of them. Jake looked around the arena. If they couldn't lift him, none of the spectators would be able to either. Then Jake spotted a cleaner, flying along on a robotic

mess sweeper. Its monster-like mouth sucked in any rubbish in its path, with the teeth catching all the dust and dirt. It was headed towards them.

'Looks like you kids need some help,' the cleaner said, hovering above them, unsmiling.

The man's long orange beard, which nearly reached to his ankles, moved up and down as he spoke. His big round stomach sat over the handles of the sweeper and when he frowned Jake couldn't even count the number of wrinkles on his forehead.

'Yes, it's our friend,' Skye stammered.

The man looked down at Henry, sitting as still as a space station in his chair. Except for his stomach, which was still pulsing. The man put his hand on Henry's stomach.

'Gob Pop. How much has he eaten?'

'A few bags' worth, I think,' Jake said. 'Is that what's wrong with him?'

'Could be.'

'Can you help him?' Skye pleaded.

'I'll scoop him onto my cleaning mobile and take him to the medical centre,' the cleaner said.

'Thanks!' Jake said. 'I'll come too.'

'No, you'd better stay here,' the man grumbled.

But Jake insisted and climbed on board. Even though he'd miss some of the Games, he wasn't going to leave Henry all on his own.

An hour later Jake was sitting inside a silver room. The walls shone like mirrors. As he moved in his chair the squeak of the legs on the shiny tiles echoed around the room. Two nursebots were just outside the room. Their metallic bodies were almost camouflaged on the silver chairs they sat on.

Jake leaned forward. Henry's eyes were still closed. The doctor placed her stethoscope on

Henry's heart. Jake hoped they would have an answer about what had happened to him soon. An engineer, standing on the other side of the bed, was looking at the panel in Henry's arm. Both the doctor and the engineer wrote something on a notepod and then placed it over the end of the bed. The writing on the pod glowed. From where he was sitting, Jake couldn't understand what it said.

'What's wrong with him?' Jake asked, worried.

The doctor spoke first, her silver gown swishing as she walked over to him. 'It's going to take some more testing to figure it out. Treating cyborgs is tricky. First, we need to know if the problem is mechanical or medical.'

The engineer joined the doctor, his silver overalls glistening. They were like two stars, only they weren't shining any light on what was going on.

'I have to agree with the doctor,' the engineer said. 'Was he having any trouble earlier in the day?'

Jake thought. There was of course the exploding popcorn, but surely that couldn't have made him shut down. Then he remembered Henry saying he'd had an upgrade. Maybe there was a problem with that. He could have short-circuited or something. Jake was just about to tell them when at that moment Henry suddenly sat up in his bed. His eyes flickered open and he started to cough up big puffy balls of Gob Pop. The doctor raced over and handed Henry a vomit tray.

'What place is this?' he said shakily when he had finished coughing up the popcorn.

'You're in the medical centre,' Jake replied. 'You froze up.'

Henry looked confused.

'During the Games,' Jake explained.

'Games? What Games?' he asked. 'And who are you?'

Jake gasped, worried Henry had lost his memory. Then the engineer walked over with a tiny microchip. He took Henry's arm and pressed the chip into the control panel before closing his arm over again. He looked up sheepishly.

'Sorry, I forgot to put his memory stick back in.'

'Where is my backpack? My popcorn is inside it. I need my Gob Pop,' Henry almost screamed.

Jake sighed in relief. He was back to normal.

'It's okay. It's in the cupboard,' Jake said.

'You need to stop eating so much. It could be what made you freeze up,' the engineer explained.

'Yes, he's right,' the doctor added. 'No more popcorn for a while, eh?'

'Can he go now?' Jake asked.

'No, he'll have to stay in for more testing. We still don't know what made him shut down.'

'We need to check on another patient. Broken leg trying to slide down the stair rails,' the doctor said, rolling her eyes, 'but we'll be back to run more tests soon. Best Henry get some rest first anyway.'

'Okay.' Jake turned to Henry. 'I'll come and check on you later.'

Jake's stomach rumbled as he left the room. He remembered that he hadn't eaten yet. He headed over to the Games cafeteria through the tunnels that connected the different sections of the arena. On the way, he thought about Henry and how he didn't have much to report back to everyone. Hopefully the doctor and the engineer would have some answers soon.

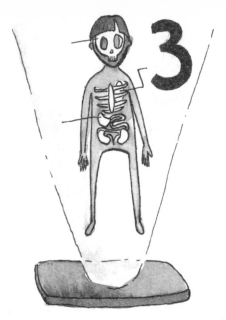

After a quick snack, Jake went to check on Henry at the medical centre. He walked up the long, echoing corridor again. He accidentally walked into the room of the kid with the broken leg but at last he found the right one. He gasped when he walked in. A crisp aluminium sheet was pulled up on the bed and there was no sign of Henry.

What had happened to him? He should have stayed by Henry's bedside. But he had thought

Henry would be okay. After all, he had woken up. What if he'd shut down again? Jake didn't even know what happened to cyborgs if they no longer worked. You couldn't just dump them like ordinary robots, could you? They were still part-human. He began to think he would never see his friend again.

'You have returned.'

Jake jumped, then turned around. He couldn't believe it. Henry walked through the door. His hair was wet from showering and a towel was slung over his shoulders. Jake had never been happier to see anyone in his life. He even almost went to hug Henry.

'Do you have any Gob Pop?' Henry asked calmly. 'It appears mine is all gone.'

Jake usually stood up for Henry when Rory got annoyed at the cyborg. This time, though, it was Jake's turn to be angry. When Henry wasn't on his bed, Jake had thought

24

for a minute that Henry might have been dead, or shut down forever – which he thought was pretty much the same thing. Jake felt himself start to shake, like a space car taking off too fast.

'Gob Pop?' Jake said sharply. 'That's all you care about?'

'What is the problem?' Henry asked, surprised.

Jake ignored Henry and stormed out of the room, smashing straight into the doctor on his way out.

'Whoa, slow down,' she said, laughing.

'Sorry,' Jake mumbled.

'Can you come with me for a moment? If you're not in too much of a hurry, that is?'

Jake was glad to leave his insensitive cyborg friend and he followed the doctor to a small room. The engineer was already sitting at a grey moon-rock table. He asked Jake to sit down.

The engineer scrolled through his notepod before stopping on a page. A 3D holographic image of Henry floated above the screen. It looked exactly like him except it was a tiny, see-through Henry. Jake could see all of his insides. He had a human heart, lungs and other organs, but there were bits of bone and intestines, and even kidneys, that looked metallic.

'Henry is a very interesting specimen,' the engineer finally said, looking up at Jake. 'How did you say you met him?'

Jake frowned at the word 'specimen'. Even though he'd been angry at Henry, his friend was more than a piece of metal. Jake also wasn't sure how to answer the question. He knew the CIA was top-secret so he probably shouldn't be telling anyone who Henry was. Not even doctors and engineers.

'Um, I met him on the Moon,' Jake mumbled.

'At Remedial Space Car Driving School.'

'Hmmm. He has very advanced technology,' the engineer said.

'His human parts work at very high levels too,' the doctor added. 'Superior brain function.'

Jake wasn't sure why they were talking like this to him.

'So, what's wrong with him?' Jake asked.

'Nothing that we can figure out. Maybe he just short-circuited.'

Jake wanted to ask whether Henry's CIA upgrade might have had something to do with it but that would let them know Henry worked for the secret agency. He decided to keep quiet.

'Can we go now?'

'Oh yes, of course,' the engineer said, shutting down the notepod. Henry's image disappeared.

'Let us know straightaway if anything else strange happens to Henry,' the doctor added.

Jake and Henry finally made it back to the arena. After letting his friends know Henry was okay, Jake quickly learned from Skye what had been happening. The event in progress was a problem-solving one. A robot from each team had to find its way to the middle of an impossibility maze. Jake hadn't missed much, though, Skye explained. The robots had been walking around in circles for almost an hour with none of them getting any closer to solving the puzzle.

Jake started to feel bored. He wasn't sure if it was from the uneventful event or because he was still worried about Henry, even if Henry *had* been rude. He thought maybe he should have told the doctor about Henry's upgrade.

Half an hour later, the green team made it right into the inner circle of the maze but then a glass wall came down and cut them off. The race kept on going. And going. *This is worse than being stuck learning space trajectories at school,* Jake thought. Rory was yawning, Milly had her eyes closed and Skye was busy creating 3D ballet routines on her notepod.

Then there was Henry. He had first thought he could solve the maze better than the robots but now seemed to have given up. He hadn't said a word. Instead, he fidgeted in his chair every few minutes. Jake almost wished Henry was still munching on his Gob Pop. At least that wasn't as annoying as him scratching his head, or shifting from side to side, or picking lint off his jumper.

'Would you stop doing that?' Jake finally snapped.

Henry stared at him as though Jake had just

slapped him in the face with a robotic hand.

'Sorry,' Jake said. 'But you are being kind of annoying.'

'I cannot stop myself from completing involuntary movement,' Henry replied.

That made Jake start to feel bad. Maybe Henry was still not right after he short-circuited.

'Do you want me to take you back to the medical centre?' Jake asked.

'No!' he said quickly. 'It is their fault.'

'Why? What did they do to you?' he said.

'They said I may not have any more Gob Pop for two weeks. That is too long.'

Jake reached under his chair and pulled out Henry's backpack. He gave Henry a packet of Gob Pop.

'Not too much, okay?' Jake said. 'We don't want you short-circuiting again.'

Henry opened the pack and poured its

entire contents into his mouth. Jake couldn't help it – he burst out laughing. Who knew a cyborg could get addicted to a snack food? But just as he began to think that Henry was fine after all, he realised he was wrong.

Henry's eyes rolled back in his head.

Henry!' Jake shouted. 'HENRY!'

Henry didn't answer. His body began jerking and his arm lit up brighter than a shooting star.

'What's happening to him?' Milly cried.

'I … I don't know!' Jake said, trying to hold Henry still.

'We have to get him back to the medical centre!' Skye said.

As if it was answering their calls, the cleaning

mobile appeared. 'I'll take him back,' the cleaner said. The mobile hovered above their heads before the cleaner lowered it down towards Henry, got it into position and scooped Henry up.

Before Jake could say anything, Henry was lifted up and carried away.

'Wow! How did he know Henry was in trouble?' Jake said aloud.

'That *was* weird,' Rory stated.

'At least we know he'll be looked after,' Skye added.

But Rory was right. How did the cleaner know that Henry needed help?

Jake soon forgot about it as the crowd around him began to cheer. He looked out to the arena. The orange team's robot had finally made it to the centre of the maze. The crowd was going wild – probably because it was over at last. Everyone settled down to watch the more exciting events.

The next event was the monster truck weightlifting. Huge eight-wheel drives were winched into the arena. This was a test of robot strength. The robot who could hold up the monster truck for the longest time would win.

The purple team was first. A huge stopwatch was shown on a floating screen. The purple robot stretched out its forklift arms and scooped up the monster truck. It held the truck for almost a minute but then the robot's metal forks began to bend under the weight. The truck fell down onto the robot's arms. A special team was brought in to disconnect the arms so the robot could leave the arena.

The green team was next. Their robot used hydraulic arms to lift the truck. Then the yellow team's robot used counterbalance with gigantic weights to hold the truck up for a record five minutes and twenty-two seconds. It was the final winner, and the scoreboard showed that

the yellow team was now leading the Games.

The robot marathon was next. It tested the battery life of the robots. Some robots started off slowly, to save energy, while others raced ahead to try to get a good lead. Jake was enjoying it so much he almost forgot about Henry. The robots finished three laps of the arena, then began the run to the arena's Games Centre. There, during the Games lunch break, they would be allowed one final charge-up before they tried to make the distance through the city in the afternoon. The huge moving screens that floated around the arena would show the robots running through the narrow streets, between skyscrapers, right through the city.

Then the computerised voice announced the Games lunch break. Before heading to one of the cafeterias, Jake and his friends stopped in at the medical centre to check on Henry. This time, when Jake tried to

35

open the big metal doors, he was surprised to find they were locked. He knocked, hard. Moments later the door was opened slightly, with a chain keeping it from opening wide. A nursebot's face appeared.

'What do you want?' she barked.

'Um, we're here to visit our friend. Henry?' Jake said, almost whispering.

The door was slammed in his face. He wasn't sure what that meant. Nursebots weren't known for being too friendly, especially to people who weren't patients. He pushed on the door but it had been locked again.

'What do we do now?' Milly asked.

'Let's get lunch,' Rory said. 'They're not going to let us in.'

'No, let's wait a minute,' Skye said.

It turned out Skye was right and a few minutes later the door opened a crack again. This time it was the doctor's face that

appeared. She looked worried.

'What's wrong with Henry?' Jake asked.

'How should I know?' the doctor snapped.

Jake was surprised that she had spoken to him that way after being so friendly earlier in the day. 'Can we go and see him?'

The doctor said nothing, just stared at the four of them with that same worried look.

'Please?' Skye added.

The doctor pursed her lips. 'I'm sorry. You can't. Come back later this afternoon.'

The door was slammed shut for the second time. Jake looked to his friends. They shrugged. No-one seemed to have any idea what was going on.

At the cafeteria they ate their meals slowly. Jake pushed his peas around. He didn't feel like eating at all. Skye put her cutlery down, her food barely touched either.

'I hope Henry's okay,' Milly said.

'Well, we can't just sit here moping about,' Skye replied.

'There's nothing we can do,' Rory argued. 'You heard the doctor. We have to wait until later.'

That may have been what they'd been told, Jake thought. But he knew better than all of them that the doctor had been acting very strangely. Earlier she had been so helpful and had even asked for his thoughts about Henry. Skye was right – there was no point moping about. They had to find out what was going on.

'Later could be too late,' Jake said, putting down his fork. 'We have to get into the medical centre and find Henry.'

'But we were told we can't see him,' Milly said.

'And it's locked up,' Skye added.

'I know a way in,' Jake said. 'We can sneak

in this afternoon, when everyone else is watching the end of the marathon. Who's in?'

Skye, Milly and Rory looked at each other. Jake knew they'd agree even before they said the word.

'Me,' they all said together.

5

ake thought it would be easy to get into
the medical centre. He had the idea of
using the side exit where the doctor and
the engineer had led him out with Henry.
But this time even the side door was firmly
locked. They went and checked the front
doors again but, as Jake had expected, they
were locked too. He tried the small diamond-
shaped windows above them. Only Milly was
small enough to fit through so he boosted her

up. No matter how hard she tried, though, the windows wouldn't open. She jumped back down.

'How are we going to get in now?' Milly asked.

Jake frowned. He was all out of ideas.

'We'll just have to wait until later, like the doctor said,' Rory said.

Jake hated to admit it but Rory was right. There was nothing else they could do. But he was worried. What if they were doing weird tests on Henry? Anything could be happening in there. Henry might be a bit annoying at times but he was also funny and smart and even seemed to care about them all – even though he was usually working for the CIA when he was with them …

'That's it!' Jake exclaimed.

'That's what?' Milly asked.

'What if the CIA sent Henry to the Games?

Maybe he's on a secret mission. I'm *sure* this all has something to do with his upgrade.'

Everyone looked at Jake like he had been playing too many real reality computer games.

'What?' he said.

'Do you know how crazy that sounds?' Rory said.

'Okay, maybe you're right,' Jake sighed, but he still thought something was up. And it had to do with Henry shutting down.

They started walking back down the connecting tube when Milly let out a little squeak. They turned. The side door to the medical centre was opening.

'Get back,' Jake hissed.

The four of them hid in the shadows. Someone in silvery overalls stepped through the open doorway. He looked left and right, and then quietly shut the door behind him. It was the engineer Jake had met earlier, and

he was carrying a metallic box under his arm. He took off down another of the tubes. Jake gestured for everyone to follow.

They tiptoed along in the shadows. It wasn't easy to be quiet walking on a metal surface. Every now and then the engineer would stop for a moment, as though sensing they were there, but they also stopped whenever he did and hid behind the pylons. Jake was already thinking of ways to explain why they were there if the engineer saw them.

At the end of the third passageway the engineer opened a red door and stepped through it, shutting the door behind him. There was a window high above the door. Rory and Jake boosted Milly up so she could look through the window. She let out a small cry of surprise.

'What is it?' Jake said, busting to find out.

'Shhh!' Milly whispered before gasping again.

Finally she reached down and tapped Jake's shoulder and the boys let her down. She looked pale.

'Well?' the other three said at once.

'It's where the robots are kept between events. Even the marathon ones are there, being recharged. They're all lined up in coloured rows. It's amazing. They're so neat, spaced out in exact rows. It looks like they measure the distance between them. They're so ...'

Jake began to get impatient. 'Yes, but what about the engineer?'

'I saw him open up his metal box. There were rows of little computer sticks in there. You know, like the ones we use for our real reality games, only smaller.'

'And?' Jake said, starting to fidget with impatience.

'He put one in each of the robots!'

'What for?' Rory replied.

44

'He's probably just getting them programmed,' Skye said. 'You know, using booster memory for the closing ceremony or something like that.'

Jake sighed. She was probably right. It seemed like a pretty normal thing for an engineer to do. Maybe they'd been having too many adventures lately to know when nothing strange was going on. He started to feel a bit silly over the whole thing. Maybe the nursebots were keeping things locked up so they could work on Henry safely – without annoying kids interrupting all the time.

Even so, the idea of going back to watch the Games wasn't so thrilling anymore.

'Let's go back,' Jake said.

They all nodded and slowly turned to go.

They got back to their seats just in time to see the marathon starting up again with the robots freshly recharged. The city street screens showed the different robots and where they were placed. It was an exciting race to watch. No-one was clearly in the lead yet. The three main leaders kept swapping and the others weren't far behind either. It was any robot's game.

But Jake couldn't concentrate properly. Neither could his friends. The four of them decided that Jake might have more luck at the medical centre if he went on his own this time. So when the robots were almost back in the arena he decided to try again.

With the sound of the roaring crowd behind him, Jake tapped on the front doors of the medical centre once more. Surely the doctor and the engineer had fixed Henry up by now. It had probably just been the Gob Pop that had messed up his system. It made sense that they hadn't wanted Jake to visit too soon. They were

probably worried Jake would give Henry more popcorn or something. After all, it was his fault Henry had shut down the second time. It had happened just after he'd given him more Gob Pop when he wasn't supposed to.

This time when the nursebot opened the door a crack, Jake smiled and said a polite 'Good afternoon.' The nursebot actually smiled back and this time closed the door carefully before going to get the doctor. A few moments later, the doctor pleasantly invited Jake inside and led him towards Henry's room.

'I'm sorry we couldn't allow you to come and visit earlier,' she said softly as they walked. 'I'm sure you understand that we needed to isolate him to make sure we sorted out the problem this time. But he can go back to the Games with you now.'

Jake felt himself blush. He'd been dreaming up all kinds of crazy things.

They walked past the room where the boy with the broken leg was resting. Two more doors up there was someone moaning, with a bandage tied around their head. Finally, they got to Henry's room.

'Ah, here we are,' the doctor said.

She opened the door to Henry's room. Henry was staring at the ceiling, looking bored. Jake cleared his throat and Henry turned to him, clearly happy to see his friend.

'Come on, Henry! Are you ready to go?'

Henry nearly leaped out of bed and Jake quickly updated him on what was happening with the marathon as they made their way to the arena. Henry seemed back to his usual self and everything felt normal again. Or was it a bit *too* normal? Jake quickly pushed that thought to the very back of his brain. He was determined to enjoy the rest of the Games.

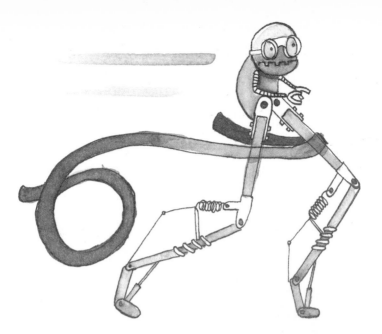

Jake had never heard a crowd go as wild as he did when the first marathon robots entered the arena. There were three laps to go. It was metal to metal between the red, blue and yellow robots. The other teams hadn't even entered the arena yet.

Amazingly, the three leaders were still running fast. As they got closer to the end they ran faster and faster until they were just three blurry streaks of colour. Then the red robot stopped suddenly on the spot. The crowd gasped.

'What's happened to the red one?' Milly asked.

'It appears it has run out of battery power,' Henry sighed.

'And so close to the end too,' Skye added, disappointed.

'I hope the blue one wins!' Jake said.

Now that the contest was between just the two robots, the crowd started to cheer louder and louder. Flashing blue and yellow flares shot across the arena like shooting stars as everyone cheered on the teams. The robots were so close together they looked like a green blur and it was hard to see which was in front. Everyone was whistling and cheering, including Jake and his friends.

But when they were just metres away from the finish line, the blue robot suddenly

stopped. There was as much booing as there was cheering. The blue team had been so close to winning and now wouldn't even finish the race! The yellow robot flashed through the finish line and then collapsed in a metallic heap. It was quickly picked up by a cleaning mobile amid the roar of the crowd.

The afternoon events continued. The robots played furious matches of metal ball, followed by deep dive and then long leap. The yellow team was still in the lead. Jake could see that there had been a reason their creators looked so shabby in the opening. They must have worked harder than space silk spider spinners to do so well in so many events.

The very last event of the afternoon was the robot wrestle. The competing robots came out into the wrestling ring wearing layers and layers of all kinds of armour. They clunked onto the field noisily. Jake was excited. This was going to be a real show of metallic strength. As he watched, though, he realised it wasn't just about strength. The robots had to get each other into holds, which wasn't easy to do when their surfaces were so slippery and shiny. He could see why the robots' armour was smooth and rounded. It made it much harder for them to grab hold of each other.

Jake watched, amazed, as the purple robot got hold of the red one. It spun it around and around in circles above its head until finally it let go. The red robot went flying like a frisbee into the crowd. Jake could hear screams as the people nearby ran to get out of the way of the incoming robot. It had been thrown so hard that its head was planted right into the back of a row of chairs. It wasn't going to be easy to get it back out again.

The two finalists were the blue and the

yellow robots again. It was a close match as they wrestled until finally the yellow robot jumped into the air and landed on the blue robot's stomach, short-circuiting it.

The Robot Games were over. The yellow team had won.

Reverse fireworks fell from the sky, covering the whole arena in rainbow-coloured glitter as the crowd clapped and whooped. Unpoppable bubbles floated in the air, changing colour as they drifted around. The faces of the robots' creators were displayed on hovering screens. The yellow team's creators looked just as grotty as they had at the beginning, with a few extra clothing stains. They were now happily celebrating, though, with streamers flapping around them. In second place were the orange robots. Their creators were still neat and clean but now wore small smiles as well.

Then the robot competitors entered the

arena again. They all made their way onto the floating ring, this time in order of placing. Each robot carried a shining flag in the colour of their team. As they waved them in the air the crowd cheered again.

Then two things happened and everything changed.

First, Jake looked over to see that Henry had shut down yet again.

Second, the robots stopped waving their flags. They held them still, their arms in the air, then dropped them.

At the same time Henry's arm panel lit up, glowing brightly under his skin.

The crowd went quiet and Jake could hear the clanging of the flags as they fell through the floating ring to the ground. The robots snaked back out and stood in one long line. Jake couldn't understand what was happening. Was this all part of the closing ceremony?

'What are they doing?' Milly whispered, frowning.

'Not sure. But it doesn't look right to me,' Jake whispered back. 'And Henry's shut down again.'

Skye looked over at Henry. He was frozen in his seat.

'What did they do to him at that medical centre?' Skye murmured, worried.

The robots shifted into formation, making eight straight rows. Suddenly they looked more like an army than Games competitors. They clicked their metal legs together and the noise echoed through the hushed arena.

Henry's arm began flashing a strange signal in dashes and dots. If he didn't already know it had stopped being used centuries ago, Jake would have thought he was sending a message in morse code.

The robots started marching on the spot,

then began to move out through the main gates of the arena. The heavy doors closed behind them – and then there was nothing. No-one moved, or spoke. It seemed it wasn't only Jake and his friends who were confused. *Is this all supposed to happen?* Jake wondered. *Or is something more sinister going on?*

A member of the crowd raced to the main entrance. She tried to open the doors but even from where Jake was sitting he could see they wouldn't budge. She yelled something out that he couldn't hear but her words quickly spread through the arena until they reached Jake's ears: 'We're locked in!'

'That can't be true,' Milly cried.

Jake stood up and watched as more and more people tried to open the doors. But the first woman had been right. No-one could open them. They had been locked inside the arena. And the robots were outside. But how?

And, most importantly, why? Jake turned to Henry. His arm was still flashing. It *had* to have something to do with the robots. But was it the work of the CIA, or was something terrible happening? He hoped it was the CIA because right now it looked like forty-nine of the most powerful robots in the solar system were under someone else's control.

Jake looked at the people who were banging on the arena's gates. Then he looked at Henry. Then he looked at the doors again. He wanted to believe it was just the Gob Pop that had short-circuited Henry. But it was too odd that Henry had started looking like his own personal disco at the very moment the robots took over. He wished Henry was activated so he could help. If anyone would know how to stop a bunch of

rogue robots it would be Henry. Right now, if the CIA really had sent Henry to stop the robot takeover, their super cyborg wasn't doing a very good job of it.

'We have to get Henry back to the medical centre. They're the only ones who can tell us what's going on,' Jake said to his friends.

'How are we going to do that?' Milly asked.

'You know we can't lift him ourselves,' Skye added.

'Pity the cleaning mobile hasn't just appeared, like it did last time,' Rory grumbled.

Jake had no idea how they were going to get Henry to the medical centre. Hover taxis weren't allowed into the arena until after the closing ceremony. 'I'm going to try and find some help,' he announced.

'I'll come with you,' Rory said. 'It's better than sitting around watching Henry flashing like a disco ball.'

'Milly and I will stay and keep an eye on him,' Skye added.

Jake nodded.

Jake and Rory edged their way around the seats. It didn't take long to run around the upper stands because most people had now squashed themselves into the arena, trying to get out. The bad part was that there was no-one around to help them carry Henry, and Jake wasn't too keen to dive into that huge crowd. He was more likely to get squashed like a space bug than find help down there.

It was also getting noisier and noisier as people started to panic. They were probably thinking they would never get out. Rory had run ahead and Jake was starting to panic too. Then Rory started yelling and pointing at something. Jake took a deep breath and ran to catch up to his friend.

Rory had stopped outside a partly opened door. Jake couldn't see anything except a thin shaft of white light beaming from the crack.

'What?' Jake cried.

'Look!' Rory said, pointing to a sign above the door.

Jake read the sign: 'Cleaner Only'.

'The cleaning mobile might be in here,' Rory cried, excitedly.

They sneaked into the room – although they didn't really need to sneak since most people were in the arena. The room was filled with every cleaning item you could imagine. There was everything from spew evaporator to robotic rubbish removal arm extensions. Then Jake spotted it. It was the cleaning mobile that the cleaner had helped them use to get Henry to the medical centre when he had short-circuited. Jake walked over to the machine.

'How does it work?' Rory asked.

Jake looked it over. 'It doesn't seem too hard to use.'

He pressed a button and the machine roared into life, loudly. It was lucky no-one was nearby. Jake climbed on board. He gestured for Rory to hop on. Rory frowned but climbed on the back. Jake turned the U-shaped steering wheel to the right and hit the accelerator. The cleaning mobile zoomed to the right, banging into the shelves and knocking containers to the floor. Jake pressed a big red button, thinking it would make the machine stop. Instead, it made the rubbish-collecting teeth start opening and closing.

'Jake! Stop this thing!' Rory shouted over the noise, trying to find a button on the back of the mobile. They whizzed around, out of control, as the sweeper collected the bottles and sponges still on the shelves, leaving a pile

of broken bits as it sucked and chomped.

Jake pressed the red button again. The jaws stopped moving and were held open wide.

'This machine isn't as easy to drive as it looks,' Jake said.

'No kidding,' Rory answered, flicking bits of sponge and cleaning foam off his shirt. 'Less accelerator, more steering this time!'

Jake shifted into reverse and accelerated slowly. He scraped the side of the door, pulling its frame loose, but finally steered them out of the room. He turned the mobile around until they were hovering just above the seating in the stands. Then he shifted into gear and very gently accelerated. Within seconds they were zipping through the arena, faster and faster, until they began knocking chairs from the stands.

'Look out!' Rory screamed as they approached an ice balls stand.

Jake pushed the controls upwards and lifted a bit higher. He was starting to get the hang of it.

Henry wasn't too hard to find, since he was still flashing away in the stands. The next tricky part was to land close enough to Henry without knocking into anyone or anything. Jake lowered the machine but came in too fast. Skye and Milly leaped away from the machine's jaws just in time as Jake stopped, hovering just beside Henry.

'Okay, I'll scoop him up.'

The girls frowned, not looking too sure he could do it. Rory jumped off the back of the mobile and helped Jake get it into position. After nearly scooping up the chair next to him, Jake finally got hold of the flashing Henry. He turned the machine around.

'I'll take him up to the medical centre,' he yelled over the roar of the machine. 'Meet me there!'

Jake took off, hoping the doctor and the engineer would have some answers. If his hunch was right, fixing Henry might solve the problem of the escaped robots too.

Jake hovered by the front doors of the medical centre but again he found that they were locked tight. He banged on the door. There was no answer. He was just about to zoom around to the side of the centre when the door opened slightly. A nursebot peered through the open crack. Her grey robot eyes rolled in their sockets when she spotted Henry. The door slammed shut. *Not again*, Jake thought. But this time he knew to wait and the doctor soon came to the door. She opened it wide to allow Jake in.

He followed her on the cleaning mobile.

'I hope you understand we had to be very careful about who we let in,' the doctor yelled over the machine. 'It's just terrible what's happened but luckily the medical centre is still running, for now.'

Jake nodded. They continued down the hallway until they reached the room where Henry had been kept last time. This time there were no other patients. All the rooms were empty and the place had an eerie feel about it. A team of nursebots entered the room.

Jake froze.

'It's okay,' the doctor said. 'The nursebots are still under our control.'

The bots lifted Henry out and placed him on the bed. They started to poke and prod at him.

'Hey! Careful with him,' Jake cried.

'Don't worry,' the doctor said. 'They're highly skilled nurses. The best of human nursing has been programmed into them.'

Jake relaxed, a little. He still wasn't happy to

see Henry being lifted and rolled and opened up.

'Come with me,' the doctor said. 'He'll be fine with the bots. You understand he has to be fully checked over first, after what's happened with the robot athletes.'

Jake nodded and followed the doctor down the silvery hallway.

'Where are the other patients?' he asked.

'They're fine,' the doctor said. 'They've all been released from the medical centre.'

Jake thought it was weird but soon they came to the small room with the moon-rock table. He followed the doctor and the engineer inside and sat down at the table again.

This time the engineer and the doctor looked at him gravely. They began to tell Jake that Henry would need closer monitoring, especially now the robot athletes had taken over. Jake asked about the robots, and the doctor and the engineer looked at each other. They started to speak but a communication screen lit up, interrupting them.

The faces of Bree and Will, the two CIA agents who looked after Henry, appeared. They sat stiffly, looking very afraid. The screen changed and the yellow wrestling robot appeared.

'This message goes out to all humans everywhere,' the robot said. 'The solar system is now under robot control. All humans have now been contained.'

'What?' Jake cried.

'Shhh,' the engineer whispered harshly.

'All buildings and houses have been locked using robotic security. There is no chance of escape. Robots are the superior beings. We will create a more effective world without the emotions of humans to interfere. Humans, you must do as your robot captors command

or face elimination.'

Jake couldn't believe what he'd just heard. It couldn't be true, could it?

The yellow robot on the screen said, 'Speak, humans.'

Bree and Will's faces appeared again.

'It's true,' Bree murmured. 'Even the CIA has been taken over. Please do as the robots say. For your own safety.'

The screen went blank. Jake knew he had to tell the doctor and the engineer everything about Henry. It was their only hope.

As quick as he could, Jake told the doctor and the engineer that Henry was really from the CIA and how he thought Henry's shutdowns and his weird flashing had something to do with the robot takeover. Maybe Henry was transmitting some kind of signal to control the robots? Jake said that he thought it must have something to do with Henry's upgrade and that the person who upgraded him might have been a

spy secretly working for the robots. When he finished speaking, the doctor and the engineer said nothing. They just stared at Jake. Then the doctor touched Jake on the arm.

'Thank you for telling us all this. We'll have the nursebots figure this out. Don't worry, it's going to be okay,' she said.

'Yes, of course,' the engineer added. 'Why don't you go to your friends and leave it to us to sort out Henry?'

Jake frowned. 'Are you sure? I could stay.'

'No!' the doctor snapped, then she smiled. 'Sorry, we're all a bit, ah, worried. But we can fix it. We just need some time. Nursebot 1132 will see you get out of here safely.'

A nursebot suddenly appeared and led Jake out of the centre before he could say any more.

Jake stood nervously on the Robot Games stage. Skye, Rory and Milly were right beside

71

him. They had all decided they needed to let everyone else in the arena know that the doctor and the engineer were going to fix everything. People were starting to get cranky as they became more worried. Some people were already fighting over food. There was an angry crowd still trying to get out of the main entrance, even though it was impossible in lockdown. They needed to know there was hope that everything would go back to normal soon. Even though Jake wasn't totally sure that Henry could be fixed to stop the robot takeover, he knew everyone had to believe it would happen.

Jake picked up the announcer's mega-microphone and switched it on.

'Um … excuse me!' Jake called into the microphone.

His voice echoed around the arena but no-one seemed to pay much attention.

'Ahem! Excuse me!' he said again.

Still everyone ignored him.

'Why don't we activate the roving screens?' Skye suggested. 'Then they'll have to notice.'

'Good idea!' Milly replied. She went with Rory to the control panel and studied the buttons for a moment. They found the right sequence and the huge screens appeared around the arena.

'They're on!' Rory said.

Jake tried speaking again, and again no-one listened. Then the screen split and the faces of the doctor and the engineer appeared.

'Your attention please,' the engineer said, his voice booming around the area.

This time everyone stopped and listened, and the engineer told the crowd what was happening. Instantly, everyone calmed down. The doctor added that Jake and his friends were helping them out. She started to ask the crowd to listen to the kids when the screen went blank. Jake took over while he still had the crowd's attention. He talked quickly about how the medical centre staff knew what the problem was and how it would be fixed very soon. They just had to be patient for a little bit longer and everything would go back to normal. He thanked everyone, hoping they had listened, and switched the microphone off.

An hour later Jake, Skye, Rory and Milly sat at a table eating a not-too-bad meal of mushy vegetables and pie. Every now and then someone would walk by and offer to help. It was amazing how everything had changed after the chaos earlier. But Jake didn't feel as confident about Henry being fixed as he had sounded.

As they ate, he talked through everything that had happened, looking for some kind of

clue about what was going on. In the end, Jake shrugged and said he didn't know why but something wasn't right at the medical centre.

Skye frowned thoughtfully over her meal, then suddenly sat up straight.

'Hang on!' she said. 'Why would the nursebots help fix Henry? This is supposed to be a *robot* takeover, right?'

'Yeah,' Rory added. 'It's weird they even let you into the medical centre.'

'And why are the nursebots doing what the doctor and the engineer want if it's the robots who are supposed to be in charge?'

'Maybe they're only pretending to help,' Milly suggested. 'Maybe they're really making sure Henry keeps transmitting signals to the other robots.'

The mushy vegetables started to feel even mushier in Jake's stomach. Skye and the others were right. It didn't make any sense that the nursebots were helping the doctor and the engineer. He knew they had to get back to the medical centre to do something – and fast.

'Oh no! I hope we're not too late,' Milly cried as they reached the medical centre.

The four of them knocked on the doors but no matter how hard they banged, this time no-one answered.

'Let's try the side door,' Skye suggested.

They ran to the other entrance, huffing and puffing, then stopped. Jake pushed gently on the door. It was unlocked. He quietly opened it and they all sneaked in silently. They tiptoed their way down the corridor, hoping to find the doctor and the engineer before the nursebots realised they were there. As they were rounding a corner Jake heard the sound of clomping feet echoing down the corridor. It was getting louder. The nursebots were

headed straight towards them.

'Quick! Hide!' he said.

The four ducked into one of the empty rooms and quickly drew the silvery blinds. Jake peeked through a gap in the blinds. Two nursebots walked straight past the room where they were hiding. As they passed, Milly accidentally knocked a metal pan off a bench. It clanged to the floor.

One of the bots stopped and the other did the same. Slowly they turned their heads.

'Did you hear that?' the first nursebot snapped.

'No!' the other answered.

The first bot looked along the corridor, turning left and right. 'My sensors don't register anything moving up or down.'

'Let's continue then. The doctor wants a new battery pack for the cyborg in thirty-one seconds, thirty, twenty-nine ...'

The bots continued on, still counting down the seconds.

'Phew, that was close,' Jake said.

'Sorry,' Milly mumbled.

'Don't worry,' Skye whispered, and the others gave her the thumbs-up.

They headed in the direction of Henry's room and when they reached it they stopped. Jake peered through the window. Henry was still flashing. One of the nursebots pulled out Henry's old battery pack and replaced it with a new one. After the changeover he flashed brighter than ever.

'That can't be good,' Skye said.

Then Jake heard a voice. He leaned in further and saw the doctor and the engineer standing there.

'Marvellous work,' the engineer said. 'I think we can rest up for a little while now.'

'Yes, good idea,' the doctor agreed.

Jake couldn't believe what he saw next. The doctor and the engineer reached into their collars and pulled up their skin. They lifted their faces over their heads.

'That's better. I couldn't see properly with that stupid skin on,' the doctor said.

Beneath their skin were metallic faces.

Robot faces.

Jake couldn't help himself. He screamed.

The robots turned sharply and looked straight at Jake. 'It's those kids. Get them!' the engineer commanded.

The nursebots moved towards the door.

'They're *all* robots!' Jake yelled at his friends. 'RUN!'

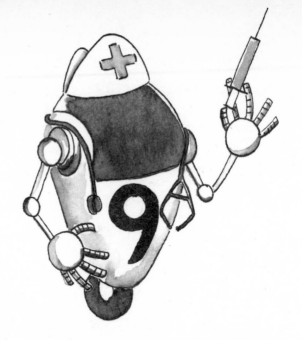

Jake, Skye, Milly and Rory raced down the corridors, skidding around corners and sliding down narrow passageways as they headed for the side door. Jake didn't waste a second looking behind him but he could hear the nursebots chasing them. The noise soon got a bit softer, though, and he began to think they could outrun the bots.

They finally reached the side door, but when Jake tried to push it open it was locked. He

banged on the door but it was no use. They were trapped. Milly screamed. Jake turned around and saw that one of the nursebots had her by the hair. The nursebot grabbed onto Rory with its other claw-like hand. The second nursebot grabbed at Jake and Skye. They struggled but the bot was too strong.

They were trapped.

The nursebots dragged the four of them down the hallway and pushed them into a room. The doctor and the engineer, now looking like their robot selves, sat at the moon-rock table. This time they didn't invite Jake to sit down with them.

'You may leave,' the engineer said to the nursebots.

They made a small bow and did as they were told.

'You can't do this,' Jake cried.

'And why not?' the doctor said calmly.

'Because humans made you in the first place.'

'Ah, that's true. But we were made better than any human. We're smarter and stronger, and we live forever. That's why humans started creating robots. We can do what you can't.'

'There's one thing we *can* do though,' Skye said angrily.

The doctor turned to her. 'And what's that?'

'We can feel things.'

The doctor laughed. 'Ha, ha. I see, that's a joke. As you can see, robots can mimic human emotion.'

'That's not the same as having real feelings.'

'Feelings aren't necessary. Now, what will we do with you lot?'

'Why don't you just let us go?' Milly said. 'The robots are in control anyway. There's not much we can do.'

The doctor seemed to be computing what

she said. 'The probability that your release would make a difference is about two point eight per cent. Not much.' She turned to the engineer. 'Can you confirm that?'

'Hmmm,' he said. He started doing his own computing. 'I get the same figure.'

Jake held his breath. *If we get out we can at least try to stop them*, he thought.

'But I'm now adding in the emotion factor and it seems they have a ninety-eight per cent chance of creating impact.'

'Ninety-eight per cent? How?' the doctor demanded.

'They seem to have a large impact on the other humans' behaviour. The crowd actually trusts these children. We cannot risk letting them go.'

Soon the nursebots came back for them. Jake and his friends were dragged into one of the empty hospital rooms and locked inside. Jake tried to force the door open but it was no use. They talked and talked about how to escape and stop the takeover but had no idea what to do. They were prisoners.

By the time it started to get dark it felt like they'd been sitting in there for hours, and Jake began to think the robots had won. They really had taken over the solar system. He was starting to feel sleepy, his head drooping onto his chest, when he heard a noise coming from outside the room. He jumped up and raced to the window. Rory and Skye followed him but Milly was already fast asleep.

Jake looked out into the corridor. The noise became louder. Then he saw it. Jaws open wide. It was the cleaning mobile, and the Games cleaner with the long beard was driving it. He came closer until he stopped right outside their door. Then he took out a diamond-shaped key and unlocked the door.

'What –' Jake started to say, but the cleaner pressed his finger to his mouth to quieten them. Skye shook Milly awake. They all climbed aboard the machine. It was a tight squeeze but by hanging onto each other they all managed to fit on the back, squashed up behind the cleaner.

'Thanks!' Jake whispered. 'How did you know where we were?'

'I guessed when I saw my cleaning mobile had disappeared,' the cleaner whispered back. 'Luckily I knew just where to come to find it – outside the medical centre.'

Jake mumbled a quiet apology. The cleaner shrugged and set the mobile in motion.

They zipped away down the corridor, out through the side door and into the connecting tunnels. The cleaner was taking them to safety but as they flew along Jake realised they were getting too far from the medical centre. They had to go back and try to stop the robots. He didn't know why but he knew they needed Henry to do it.

'We have to turn back and get Henry,' Jake called over the machine.

'It's too risky,' the cleaner argued.

'Getting Henry is the only way we're going to stop the machines. I know it.'

'We'll get caught,' the cleaner said.

'He's right. We have to stop the robots,' Skye agreed.

The cleaner still refused to stop. Jake called for the others to hang on to each other. He had a crazy idea but there was no other way. On the count of three he pushed the cleaner from the cleaning mobile and the man fell, landing on the floor of the tunnel. Jake whipped the mobile around and headed back in the other direction. He looked over his shoulder to see the cleaner brushing himself off and waving his fist in the air angrily. Jake mouthed a 'Sorry' to him and kept going. He knew they would make it back to Henry now. He just hoped they weren't too late.

The cleaning mobile stopped at the far end of the hall where Henry's room was. They'd quickly come up with a plan for Skye to go ahead of them and distract the nursebots. Once the nursebots took off after Skye, they would race in and grab Henry on the mobile. Jake just hoped the plan would work.

Skye jumped down and started running down the hallway. Jake could see that the nursebots were sitting on plastic chairs outside Henry's room. Their eyes were closed – they were in sleep mode. Skye was nearly past them when the bots' motion detectors finally woke them. Their heads snapped forward and their eyes opened but it still took a moment for them to work out what was happening. Skye took the chance to get a safe distance ahead of them.

When they realised what was happening the bots rose from their chairs. Skye ran faster down the hallway. The bots chased after her. It looked like the plan was actually going to work.

With the bots gone, Jake flew the mobile into Henry's room and they got him safely on board. Jake could see the bots had nearly caught up to Skye so he let out a loud whistle. They stopped suddenly and turned. Jake pointed to Henry. The bots ran back towards them and the cleaning mobile took off.

It was easy for them to beat the bots on the machine and it wasn't long before they were safely out of the medical centre. They zoomed around the other side of it. Skye raced out the side door, red-faced and puffing. They scooped her up as they passed and flew towards the Games cafeteria. Jake looked at Henry. He was still deactivated, and the flashing on his arm showed that strange signal of dots and dashes. He tried to remember what he had learned about code in history class. But no matter how hard he thought he just couldn't figure out what it meant. All he knew was Henry had something to do with the robot takeover and if they didn't figure out what it was soon, humans could end up being under the control of robots forever.

They reached the cafeteria but a large silver bolt had been placed across the door handles. They were locked out.

'What do we do now?' Milly cried.

'Leave it to me,' Jake said.

Jake opened up the jaws of the mobile and moved the machine forward. He clamped the jaws down around the bolt and then reversed hard. The bolt bent and snapped in two. The doors opened and they flew inside. In the cafeteria, Jake quickly scooted the mobile over to a corner and slid Henry onto a row of chairs, laying him down across them. They huddled over him, staring helplessly at their cyborg friend, his arm still flashing. No-one knew what to do with him.

'We need to figure out why the robots need Henry for the takeover,' Skye said.

'It has to have something to do with his upgrade,' Jake said.

'All they did back at the CIA was give him a new panel and a cap,' Rory argued.

'And it's his panel that's flashing like a disco ball,' Jake said. 'That has to be it. If only we could work out the code.'

'I've got it!' Skye said.

'You know the code?' Rory said, surprised.

'No. But he got a new panel, which has something to do with it. And a new –'

'– cap!' Jake yelled. 'You're a genius, Skye.'

He pulled off Henry's cap. But when he removed it he found nothing inside it. It was just an ordinary cap. He tossed it aside, annoyed. Then he felt Skye tap him on the shoulder. He turned. A short wire was poking straight out of the top of the cyborg's head.

'What *is* that?' Milly cried.

'I don't know,' Jake said, 'but I do know he's never had anything sticking out of his head before.'

Though Jake had never seen it before he knew it looked familiar. He thought back to his history books again. This time he remembered where he'd seen that kind of wire. In the old days, before real reality toys, there were remote-control toys – boats, planes and cars. The wire was an antenna. Henry was controlling the robots via remote control! And if Henry was the transmitter that meant the robots were the receivers. The flashing on

Henry's arm had to be some kind of signal, telling them how to act. He remembered seeing the engineer putting the USB sticks into each of the robots. The robots' normal programs must have all been changed over.

Jake told the others what he thought.

'So we need to stop the transmission,' Rory said. 'But how?'

'Even though Henry is shut down, he's still transmitting the signals,' added Milly.

'Let's think back to what we learned at school,' Jake said. 'What else does a remote-control toy need?

'A person to control it,' Skye suggested.

'Yes. We already know the doctor and the engineer are controlling him. There must be something else.'

They all thought hard but no-one came up with anything.

'We're running out of time. The nursebots

will find us soon and they won't be happy, Rory said nervously.

Just as he said those words Jake saw six jet-powered nursebots heading through the cafeteria doors, and they were moving straight towards them.

'What are we going to do?' Milly yelled.

They still didn't know how to stop Henry's transmissions. They crouched over Henry as the bots flew towards them. The first nursebot grabbed Milly and took off with her. The others took hold of Jake, Skye and Milly. No matter how hard they struggled, they couldn't get away from the bots. Soon Jake found himself zooming out of the cafeteria and down the connecting tunnels. Behind him he could see Henry being carried by two of the bots as well.

They soon landed back at the medical centre and Jake felt his mouth go as dry as the

Moon's surface. The bots dropped them at the end of a long corridor, and at the other end the doctor and the engineer appeared. They didn't look happy as they stamped straight towards them. The engineer was holding a small rectangular object in his hand.

Jake looked at Henry. The flashing lights on Henry's arm were starting to fade. Jake looked again at the object in the engineer's hand.

'It's power!' he whispered excitedly, so the nursebots wouldn't hear.

'What?' the others mouthed.

'The other thing that's needed for remote control. A power source!'

'Yes!' Skye hissed. 'That's why they kept Henry in the medical centre. His battery needs to be charged for the transmissions to work!'

They had only seconds until the engineer reached them. Jake quickly opened up the panel in Henry's arm before the nursebots could grab him. He ripped out the battery pack, tore off its cover and threw it as hard as he could towards the far wall of the corridor. It smashed open and pieces clattered to the floor.

'Nooooo!' the engineer screamed.

That was the last thing he said as he stopped, his arm still outstretched and his robotic hand holding the battery. He was frozen. The same thing happened to the doctor. She stopped moving just steps behind the doctor. The nursebots fell in a metal heap beside them.

'We did it!' Jake screamed.

Jake and his friends didn't have to wait long before the sleek, steely CIA craft came in to land. The agents stepped out, looking tired and happy at the same time. They made their way over to the group.

'Thank goodness you figured it out,' Will said.

'Yes, without you we would have been robot-run forever,' Bree added. 'Not even the CIA could override them once we were under their control.'

'You knew all along that the robots were planning to take over?'

'No! We only knew that the medical centre was suspicious, which is why we sent Henry on this mission with you,' Will explained.

'We didn't know they were all robots inside. Or that they had planned to take over the whole solar system,' Bree explained.

Jake glanced over at the still body of Henry. 'I think there's someone you might have forgotten.'

The agents looked guiltily over at Henry.

'Of course. Poor Henry. We'll have our agents restore him immediately,' Will stammered.

A junior agent appeared from inside the craft, carrying a rectangular box. It was completely see-through so it looked more like a window than a briefcase. Inside were all kinds of tools Jake had never seen before. The agent took out a slim object with a small

rounded end. She bent over Henry and placed the tool over the top of Henry's head. She twisted it around until the transmitter in the top of Henry's skull popped out.

'He'll need some head repair and hair implants,' she said, frowning at the bald spot on the top of Henry's head.

'Yes, we'll worry about that later,' Will snapped.

Jake smiled at the agent. She nodded and quickly worked on reactivating Henry. First, she took out the panel that had been flashing in his arm and replaced it with the old version. Then she reinserted a fresh battery pack and closed his arm back over.

'Let's see if he works okay,' she said, switching him back on.

Henry's eyes snapped open. He looked right then left. He seemed a bit confused about where he was. Then he spoke.

'Where is my Gob Pop?'

'You haven't fixed him properly,' Will grumbled.

Jake and his friends just laughed.

'What?' Will said.

Between giggles, Skye explained, 'He's perfectly normal. He's been a bit, um, hooked on Gob Pop.'

'Oh, I guess we'd better sort that out back at CIA headquarters,' Bree said.

'Well, it's time to get these rogue robots out of here,' Will said, glancing at the doctor and the engineer.

'What will happen to them?' Milly asked.

'They'll be reprogrammed. All the robots will be.'

'Here, I nearly forgot. Before we round up the robots. I have something for you,' Bree said.

The agent held out a shimmering envelope. Jake took it and opened it up. Inside, four

tickets glowed red as lava. He looked at the agents with surprise.

'You deserve something special for what you've done,' Bree said.

Jake couldn't believe it. They all had tickets for them and their families to stay at the Floating Hotel of Venus. Hardly anyone got to stay there – unless they were *really* famous. It was the most amazing place in the solar system, or so he had heard. He laughed.

'Wow! Thanks.'

'Ah, you're *sure* it's not secretly another mission?' Skye asked.

Bree laughed. It sounded a bit fake to Jake but she insisted it was just for them to have some fun.

'We couldn't have done it without you. We had no idea that upgrade on Henry was done by a spy at our headquarters. He seemed so ... so genuine,' Bree said.

'I bet he'll be locked up in prison for a very long time,' Skye said.

Bree and Will just looked at each other.

'Ah, well ...' Bree stammered.

'You haven't caught him, have you?' Jake said.

'He won't be too hard to find,' Will said, sounding unsure. 'Not with that long orange beard.'

The others all looked at each other.

'Long orange beard?' Rory said.

'The cleaner!' they said together.

The friends raced away, dragging Henry with them before the agents knew what was happening.

Jake and his friends raced to the cleaner's room, hoping to catch up to him in time. When they arrived the door was half open. They stepped inside but the cleaner wasn't there.

'We're too late!' Milly cried.

Jake thought hard. There was only one other place he could think of where the cleaner might go.

'Follow me!' he yelled.

Jake raced towards the medical centre, his friends following behind him. He ran by the side entrance, sped down the connecting tube and kept on going until he reached the end of the third passageway. The red door was wide open. If his hunch was right, the cleaner would try to make his escape from the robot holding bay.

Jake looked around the now empty bay. It was quiet and dark. Maybe the cleaner hadn't come here. Or maybe they were too late and he'd already escaped. Then he heard it – a whirring noise that sounded a lot like the cleaning mobile's engine.

'There!' Skye cried.

Jake had been right. The cleaner was aboard the mobile. They ran over to him but he hovered above them, out of reach.

'It was you who implanted the transmitter in Henry,' Jake yelled over the roar of the machine.

'And it was *you* who ruined all my plans,' the cleaner barked back. 'It was meant to be so easy. I put the transmitter in Henry, pretending it was an upgrade. Next, I inserted the antenna and gave him a fancy cap to hide it. Finally, I gave him enough Gob Pop to make him short-circuit so he would shut down and could then be remote-controlled. Then, quite simply, by controlling all the robots, I would finish my plans of taking over the solar system.'

'That's why you told me to never take the special cap off,' Henry said.

'But what about the doctor and the engineer?' Jake said. 'How did you control them?'

'Ah, smart boy,' the cleaner sneered. 'They were the trickiest part. It's not easy to mess with such scientific programs. Much harder than simple robots. And I had to make it so that everyone would think the robotic doctor and the engineer were behind the takeover.'

'So, how did you do it?' Skye asked, frowning.

'It was easy in the end. I did the same with them as I did with the other robots. But I also inserted a special program that made them tell you they were behind the takeover. That way no-one would ever suspect it was me, a simple cleaner.'

'But why?' Jake asked.

'Do you think it's fun cleaning up after a bunch of grotty spectators? I was made for bigger things than sweeping and taking out the rubbish. Now, I'm sorry kids, but I gotta fly.'

He'll never be able to escape the arena in

that cleaning mobile, though, Jake thought. He didn't even have a space suit on. He wouldn't last five seconds out in space in the open machine. But then the back of the mobile started to move. Like a convertible, a clear dome came over the top of the mobile, closing the cleaner safely inside. The cleaner grinned at them from inside and waved goodbye.

'Oh no!' Milly cried, 'We'll never stop him now.'

The mobile moved over towards the exit doors. The doors opened up and Jake knew they were only moments away from letting him escape.

'I thought he was being nice to me, giving me that cap and Gob Pop,' Henry stated. 'I will not let him get away.' Henry stomped over to a panel beside the exit doors as the cleaning mobile hovered above him. He entered a code as the first set of doors opened and the

cleaner entered the airlock chamber. They started to close behind him. When they were shut Henry pressed another button.

'There!' he said. 'He's locked in. He won't be going anywhere now.'

'Good job Henry,' Rory said.

Henry beamed. Rory hardly ever said anything nice to the cyborg.

It didn't take long before the CIA agents had tracked Henry and arrived at the scene. Bree and Will looked surprised to see the kids had captured the robot takeover mastermind.

'Good work!' Bree uttered.

Will motioned for Henry to open up the doors. As they opened up the top of the machine, Bree and Will and the junior agent pulled the cleaner from the escape pod.

'You're coming with us,' Will said, handcuffing him.

'Oh, and here's your Gob Pop,' Bree said,

holding a bag out to Henry. 'You deserve it.'

Henry shook his head and pushed the bag away.

'I believe I will give it up,' Henry said.

'Good idea,' Skye chimed in.

While the CIA agents took the cleaner away in their space craft, Jake and his friends walked out the front gates of the arena. The space car park was nearly empty now, so they could all watch Jake's dad nearly smash into the wall trying to park. Jake grimaced at his friends, who were laughing.

'See you on Venus,' he said.

They waved goodbye and Jake walked up to the car.

'Jake!' his mum said. She jumped out of the car and squashed him in a big hug. Finally, she let go. 'We were so worried about you when the robot takeover happened. How lucky that you were safe inside the Games arena!'

Jake climbed in, smiling to himself. If only she knew.

ABOUT THE AUTHOR

Candice's quirky style, fast-paced narratives and originality appeal to reluctant boy readers in particular.

Following several years working in the media, Candice now devotes her time to her writing and to raising her two young daughters. She is also a Literacy Champion for the Municipal Literacy Partnership Program (MLPP).